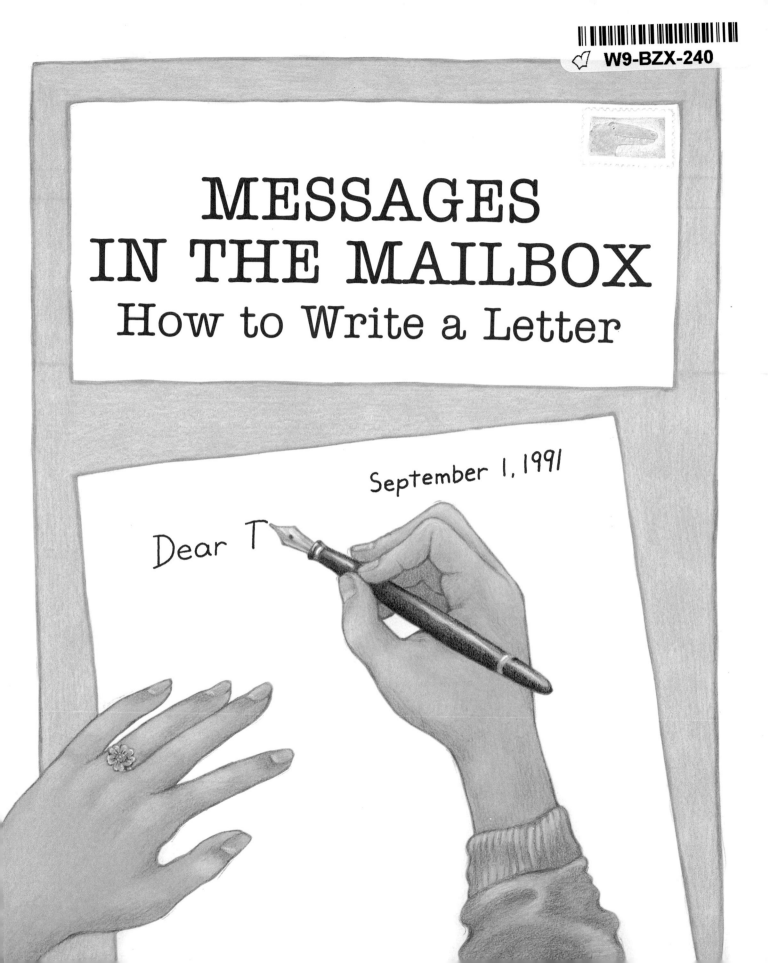

MESSAGES IN THE MAILBOX
How to Write a Letter

September 1, 1991

Dear T

September 1, 1991

Dear Readers,
 I hope you will enjoy this book. It will help you to stay in touch. Why not write a letter to someone today?

Fondly,
Loreen J. Leedy

MESSAGES
IN THE MAILBOX

How to Write a Letter

written and illustrated by

LOREEN LEEDY

Holiday House / New York

To all my pen pals

Library of Congress Cataloging-in-Publication Data
Leedy, Loreen.
Messages in the mailbox : how to write a letter /
written and illustrated by Loreen Leedy.
p.   cm.
Summary: Discusses the different kinds of letters,
the parts of a letter, and who can be a potential
correspondent, and provides examples.
ISBN 0-8234-0889-2
1. Letter-writing—Juvenile literature.   [1. Letter writing.]
I. Title.
BJ2101.L44 1991   91-8718   CIP   AC
395′.4—dc20
ISBN 0-8234-1079-X (pbk)

FRIENDLY LETTERS

I can write to my best friend who moved away!

I'll write to my cousin!

I'll write to my uncle!

Great! Here is what a friendly letter looks like . . .

HEADING

504 Jungle Lane
Swampland, FL 32707
September 15, 1999

SALUTATION

Dear Grandma Gator,

BODY

Hello! How are you? I hope your tail is feeling better.

My students are learning about letters, and they are writing to all sorts of different people. One of them even wants to write to the President! They are excited to know they can get in touch with almost anyone!

CLOSING

Much love,

SIGNATURE

Alice

POSTSCRIPT

P.S. I forgot to mention my new pet snake, Fifi.

Start with the *heading*. Write your street address, city, state, zip code, and the date in the upper right corner.

The *salutation* is a greeting that reads: Dear (fill in the blank),

The *body* is the main part of the letter that tells what you have to say.

If your friend already knows your address, just put the date in the *heading*.

Use a pen on plain paper for a simple, friendly letter.

"Sincerely" is one *closing*. Can anyone think of others?

Your friend!

Love!

Best wishes!

See you soon!

Hugs and kisses!

Much love, Alice

For the *signature*, just sign your name.

If you think of something to add at the end, just write *P.S.* (for *postscript*), and finish.

P.S. I fo

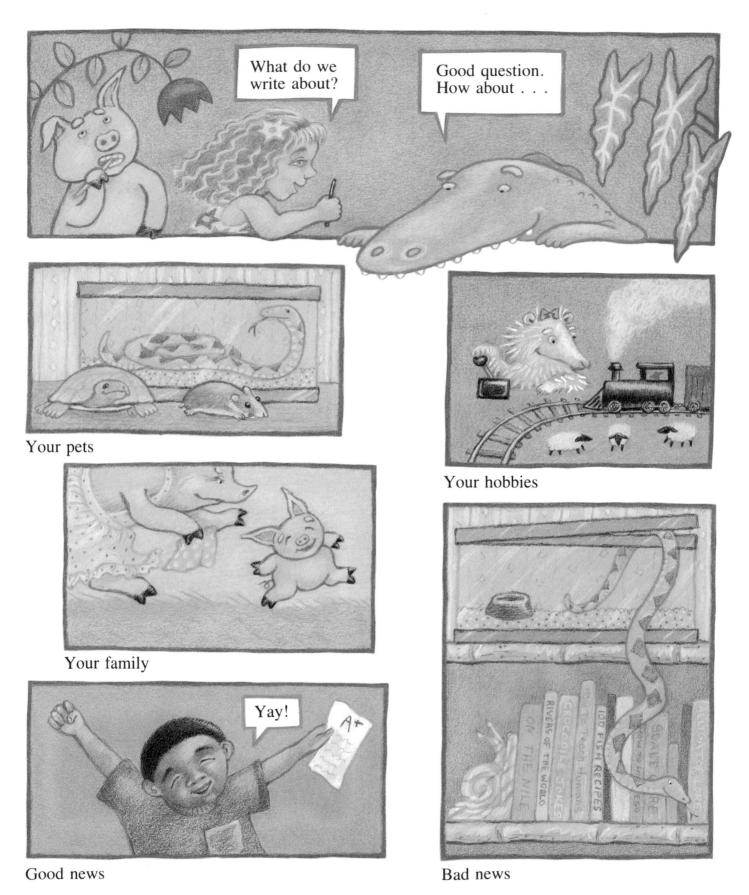

Your pets

Your hobbies

Your family

Good news

Bad news

A pen pal from another country

A neighbor

Relatives

A teacher

Famous people

9

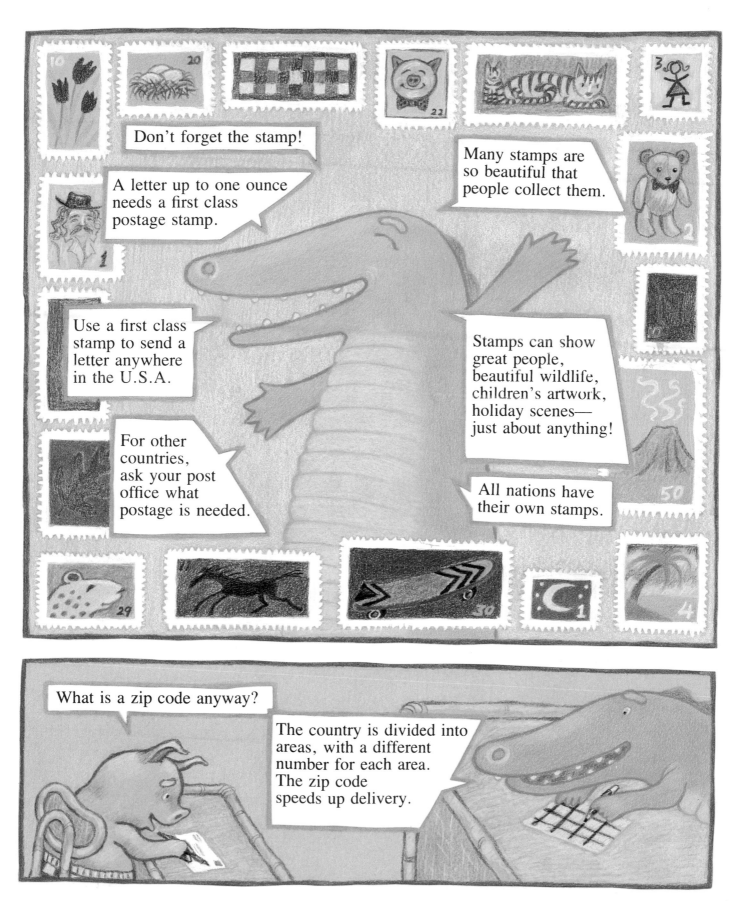

CUT A SHAPE   Cut construction paper or typing paper into shapes to write on:

 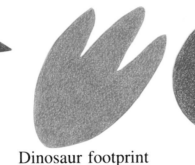 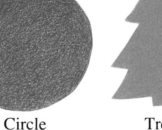

House   Dinosaur footprint   Circle   Tree   Swamp thing

DRAW A PICTURE   Make a painting or drawing. Use the back of the paper for writing a letter.

MAKE A PUZZLE   Write a letter and cut it up with scissors. Put pieces in an envelope and mail.

INVISIBLE INK

1. Write a letter with a regular pen, but leave plenty of space between each line.

2. Use a toothpick dipped in lemon juice to write the secret message between lines. Let dry, then mail the letter.

3. Your friend can iron the letter (with adult permission), and the heat will make the invisible ink appear.

Dear Juan,
Hi! How are you?

Are you going

to the game?

See you,
Brad

Dear Juan,
Hi! How are you?
MEE—
Are you going

to the game?

See you,
Brad

Dear Juan,
Hi! How are you?
MEET ME
Are you going
BEHIND THE
to the game?
GYM AT 8:00.
See you,
Brad

POSTCARDS

When you are traveling, it is fun to send postcards to friends and family. Pick postcards that show where you are, and write a few lines about your adventures. Don't write anything private, because anyone can read a postcard.

Dear Kim,
We went on a boat under the waterfall and got soaked. We made a campfire to dry out and ate hot dogs and marshmallows. Wish you were here! See you soon.
Your friend,
Sarah

Kim Kong

27 Jaguar Rd.

Swampland, FL

32707

INVITATIONS

If the invitation says *R.S.V.P.*, you should call or write a note letting the host or hostess know if you can attend. (The words "regrets only" mean to get in touch only if you can't attend.)

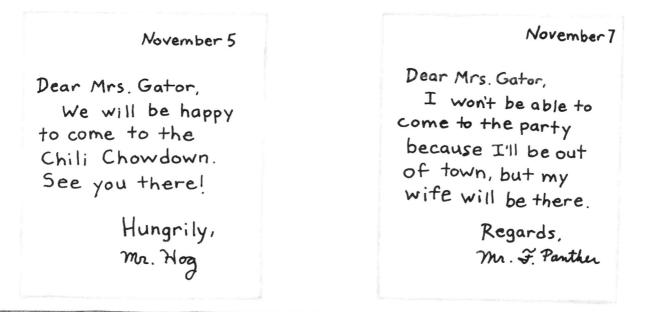

November 5

Dear Mrs. Gator,
    We will be happy to come to the Chili Chowdown. See you there!

    Hungrily,
    Mr. Hog

November 7

Dear Mrs. Gator,
    I won't be able to come to the party because I'll be out of town, but my wife will be there.

    Regards,
    Mr. F. Panther

THANK-YOU NOTES

It is very important to thank friends and relatives for gifts they have mailed you.

Right! Write how much you enjoy the gift, and if it was money, explain what you plan to do with it.

That way they'll know we got it.

If they never heard from you, their feelings would be hurt.

12/29/99

Dear Great Grammy,
    Thank you for the sweater you knit for me. It fits perfectly, and everybody says it looks pretty on me.
        I love you!
        Kim

It's polite to write a short note if you have been a guest overnight in someone's home.

1/3

Dear Mrs. Green,
    Thank you so much for having me stay at the ranch. I liked feeding the chickens, but the best part was riding the ponies. I'm not sore anymore!
        Sincerely,
        Sarah

GET-WELL LETTERS

People like to get mail when they are sick at home or in the hospital.

They want to know what is going on in the outside world.

You look kind of sick!

I was in the hospital once.

January 10, 2000

Dear Dave,
   I'm sorry you aren't feeling well. We miss you. With your nose, your cold must be a whopper!

See you soon,
Juan

If you are the one who is sick, you probably have time to write a few letters yourself.

1/12

Dear Juan,
   I still have a few sniffles, but the doctor says I'll be better by next week. That's good news, because I'm almost out of tissues.

Your friend,
Dave

LOVE LETTERS

SYMPATHY LETTERS

It is very sad when someone dies.

The family needs the comfort of letters from friends and relatives.

February 5, 2000

Dear Sarah,
   I was so sorry to hear that your grandpa died. He was fun to talk to when he came to your house. Please give my sympathy to your family.

Sincerely,
Kim

NOTES OF APOLOGY

Did your dog dig up the neighbor's garden?

Did your home run shatter a window?

Did you call your best friend a mean name?

A letter of apology can help make things right again.

March 1, 2000

Dear Mrs. Jones,
   I'm sorry my brother dug up your flowers. I accidentally left the gate open.
   I'm going to mow lawns to earn enough money to pay for the damage.

Your neighbor,
Sammy Fox

CONGRATULATIONS

FORM LETTERS

Lots of wonderful things have happened to me, and I have lots of wonderful friends! How can I tell everybody my good news?

You can write one letter and mail it to everybody!

Some people fit a year's worth of news into one letter.

---

501 Panther Path
Swampland, FL 32707
December 15, 1999

Dear Lisa,

So much has happened this year—most of it good! I spent a week on a ranch and got to ride a pony.

We have a great class in school, and we've had lots of fun. We had a chili party, and we write letters to lots of different people. Our teacher is an alligator, but she's nice!

My family went on vacation to Foamy Falls, which was beautiful. My dad pretended to fall off the boat, but he didn't really! Write me!

Fond regards,
Sarah

P.S. Lisa—I like Sammy Fox, and I think he likes me too!!! S.

Type or neatly handprint a letter with all the news. Leave the name blank in the *salutation*.

Photocopy as many letters as you need.

Write in each person's name, sign the letter, and add a personal *P.S.*, if you like.

Address each envelope, put the letter inside it and seal, stamp, and send it. (See page 10 to learn more about addressing a letter.)

FAN LETTERS

303 Muddy Way
Swampland, FL 32707
April 2, 2000

Dear Miss Splendid,

I think you are the best singer in the whole world. I play your songs all the time, and know all the words. Are you ever going to have a concert in Swampland, Florida?

Your fan,
Sammy Fox

707 Quicksand St.
Swampland, FL 32707
October 27, 1999

Dear Captain Flash,

I really like your Space Cops show, and I watch it every week (even the reruns!) The different aliens are so cool. I liked the one with the electric feathers. Could I have your autograph? Thank you!

Sincerely,

Brad Johnson

May 5, 2000

Dear Mrs. Gator,

You may not be famous, but I'm a fan of yours! I have fun in class every day, because we always do new things. I have learned a lot, and I'm going to be a teacher when I grow up.

Your student,
Missy

Famous people get lots of mail, so you may not get an answer. But you might!

BUSINESS LETTERS

A business letter is a little different because it's more formal. Here's one style you can use.

Use a typewriter or neatly hand print on plain white 8½″ × 11″ paper.

HEADING

Alice Gator
Swampland School
500 Jungle Lane
Swampland, FL 32707

October 21, 1999

INSIDE ADDRESS

Robert Baloney
Edible Toy Company
2001 Banana Street
Appleton, VT 05039

SALUTATION

Dear Mr. Baloney:

BODY

I am a teacher, and my students would like to raise money for some special projects. We think your licorice locomotives, peppermint pogo sticks, and chocolate chipmunks would sell well. Will you please send us a price list and samples?

Also, is it possible to special order some candy in the shape of our school mascot, a snapping turtle? Thank you.

CLOSING
SIGNATURE

Sincerely,

Alice Gator

Alice Gator

The *inside address* has the person's name, the organization's name, the street address, city, state, and zip code on the left.

The business *salutation* has a colon for punctuation.

Dear Mr. Baloney:

Here are some business *closings*.

Always use titles!

Mr. (married or single man)

Ms. (married or single woman)

Mrs. (married woman)

Miss (unmarried woman)

Dr. (man or woman who is a doctor)

Sincerely,

Best wishes,

Cordially,

Regards,

If you don't know the person's name, use ''To Whom It May Concern'' as the *salutation*.

Use your first and last name for the *signature*.

Use a long (9½″ × 4¼″) envelope and fold the letter like this:

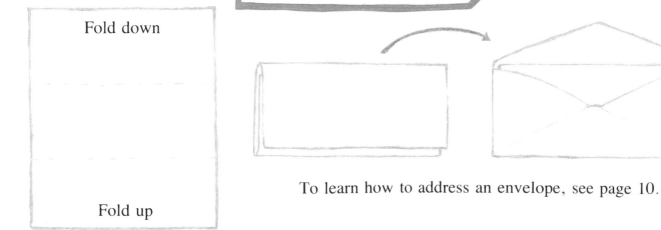

Fold down

Fold up

To learn how to address an envelope, see page 10.

REQUESTS

707 Quicksand St.
Swampland, FL 32707
November 1, 1999

Space Cops Show
3030 Starlight Blvd.
Los Angeles, CA 90909

To Whom It May Concern:

I am interested in getting a Space Cops Jet Pack, but I can't find one in the stores here. Would you let me know how to get one?

Space Cops is my favorite show!

Sincerely,

Brad Johnson

Brad Johnson

COMPLAINTS

707 Quicksand St.
Swampland, FL 32707
November 19, 1999

Space Cops Stuff, Inc.
1717 Shoddy Street
Los Angeles, CA 90909

To Whom It May Concern:

I bought a Space Cops Jet Pack from you, but it doesn't work right. It just hops once or twice, then it starts beeping. Would you please refund my money or send me a new Jet Pack? I will return the broken one.

Thank you.

Cordially,

Brad Johnson

Brad Johnson

PROTESTS

707 Quicksand St.
Swampland, FL 32707
November 30, 1999

The Honorable Jane Long
United States Senator
Senate Office Building
Washington, D.C. 20543

Dear Senator Long:

I'm writing because of a problem I had with the Space Cops Stuff Co. in Los Angeles, CA. They sold me a Space Cops Jet Pack that doesn't work, and they won't give me a refund or a new one.

I don't think it's fair for this company to take money for a bad product, and I wanted to let you know. Thank you.

Sincerely,

Brad Johnson

Brad Johnson

LETTERS TO THE EDITOR

707 Quicksand St.
Swampland, FL 32707
December 30, 1990

The Swamp Crier
99 Mangrove Way
Swampland, FL 32707

Dear Editor:

Earlier this year, I bought a defective toy from a store in California. They would not replace it or return my money. I wrote our senator and her office was able to convince the company to replace the toy.

I saw your article about consumer problems, and I thought your readers would like to know—it pays to speak up!

Sincerely,

Brad Johnson

Brad Johnson

MAILING LETTERS

MAILBOXES

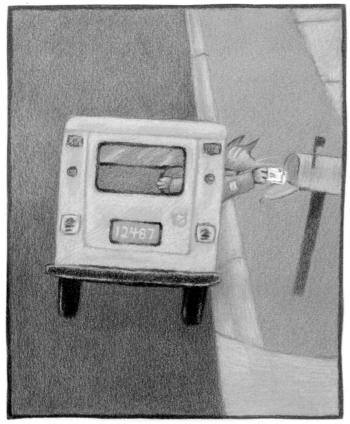

LETTER CARRIER

POST OFFICE

Everybody loves to get mail.

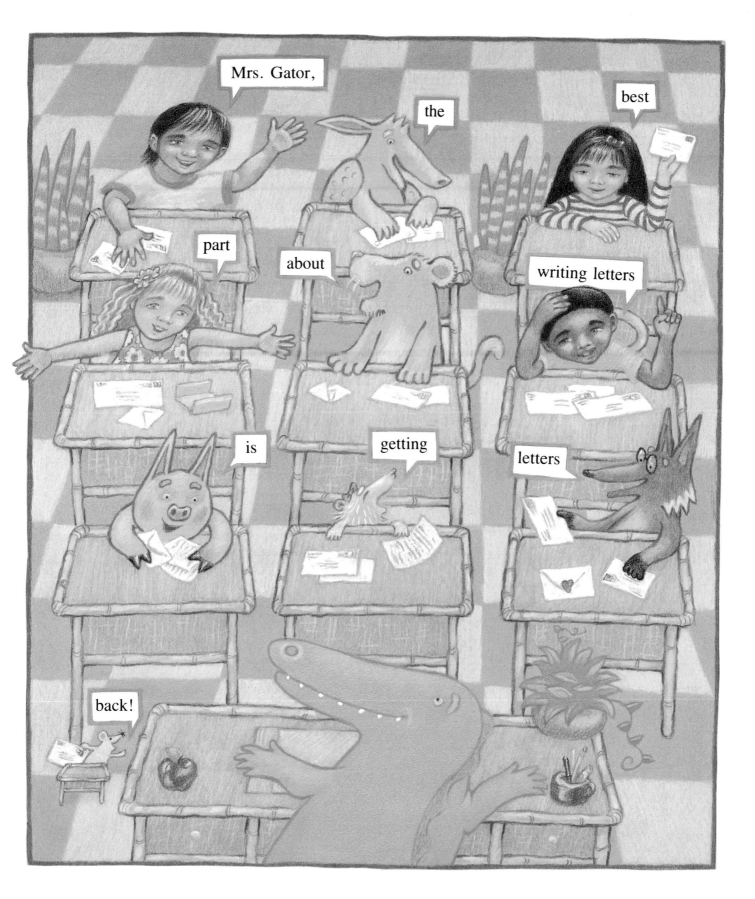

STATE AND TERRITORY ABBREVIATIONS

AL	Alabama		MO	Missouri
AK	Alaska		MT	Montana
AS	American Samoa		NE	Nebraska
AZ	Arizona		NV	Nevada
AR	Arkansas		NH	New Hampshire
CA	California		NJ	New Jersey
CO	Colorado		NM	New Mexico
CT	Connecticut		NY	New York
D.C.	District of Columbia		NC	North Carolina
DE	Delaware		ND	North Dakota
FL	Florida		OH	Ohio
FM	Federated States of Micronesia		OK	Oklahoma
GA	Georgia		OR	Oregon
GU	Guam		PA	Pennsylvania
HI	Hawaii		PR	Puerto Rico
ID	Idaho		PW	Republic of Palau
IL	Illinois		RI	Rhode Island
IN	Indiana		SC	South Carolina
IA	Iowa		SD	South Dakota
KS	Kansas		TN	Tennessee
KY	Kentucky		TX	Texas
LA	Louisiana		UT	Utah
ME	Maine		VT	Vermont
MD	Maryland		VA	Virginia
MA	Massachusetts		VI	Virgin Islands
MH	Marshall Islands		WA	Washington
MI	Michigan		WV	West Virginia
MN	Minnesota		WI	Wisconsin
MP	Northern Miriana Islands		WY	Wyoming
MS	Mississippi			